SIXTEEN STORIES

SIXTEEN STORIES

Contemplatives in Action

MARIO NACINOVICH

Published by Tablo

Publisher and wholesale enquiries: orders@tablo.io

20 21 22 23 LSC 10 9 8 7 6 5 4 3 2 1

Table of Contents

This book is dedicated to Rev. William J. O'Malley, S.J. who once shared,
"The question is not whether life is difficult or not. That is a given.
The question is whether you're going to try and solve it or just sit there and
moan about it."

Salt-aired scrap

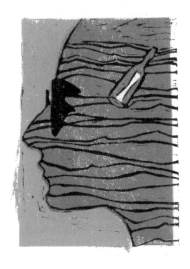

My mouth was completely parched. I was far too tired and chafed at that point in the day to want to get up from my reclined vantage point in the construction of the world's greatest sandcastle with my nephews. The afternoon sun was shaded from my eyes thanks to my camouflage jungle hat and the scent of my third application of sunscreen was also most certainly causing some mild hallucinations when I first saw the glimmer across the water's edge. I at first dismissed the thought of getting up, thinking it was some random ray of sunshine reflecting off the surface water at just the precise angle. Squinting through my sand- and salt-encrusted sunglasses, I recognized that familiar bob and weave of the glassware – it was a bottle. As I approached the weathered object in its solo interpretive dance, there was the all but now cliche image of a glass bottle with cork on its top and what clearly looked like a rolled up piece of paper inside.

I picked up this aquatic antique, andged to pry the top off with ease but struggled to reach this ultra rare "scroll". My digitus secundus manus and digitus med'ius (index and middle fingers) were simply too large and lacked the dexterity to navigate such a delicate extraction. Without wasting any time, I knew I had to recruit my youngest nephew John Paul into this mission.

Johnny is all boy – while he's the most rugged four year old ever assembled, he has a curious eye for assisting in such precise maneuvers. With the ease of an otolaryngologist removing a foreign object from deep in an ear canal, Johnny grasped the tightly curled yellowed paper, shrugged his sunburnt shoulders, handed me the insubstantial sheet, and went back to erecting his golden sandy stronghold. With no premonition of what I could possibly read, I unfurled this single paged treasure.

The page was well worn and barely interpreted the 187 on the top left corner of the page. I could make out some of the words near the middle of the page that read, "All right. Listen to me a minute now....I may not word this as memorable as I'd like to, but I'll write you a letter about it in a day or two. Then you can get it all straight." The edges of the page were tattered and bleached from the sun. Nearly all of the remaining words and letters on this salt-aired scrap were obscured.

I wondered for about seventeen seconds what was the intent of the hopeless romantic who had launched this into the Atlantic. I didn't want to waste any more time contemplating its origins or the proclivities of its previous owner – the spirits moved me to just turn the page over.

My eyes could barely make out 188 on the top left of this page and the word "Rye" near the middle. Near the center of this side of this ancient seafaring artifact, I deciphered what appeared to be another quote, "Here's what he said: 'The mark of the immature man is that he wants to die nobly for a cause, while the mark of the mature man is that he wants to live humbly for one.'"

What had begun as a late afternoon adventure into the finer details of fabricating a beach fare foundation and fortress, led to a walk back into time and reintroduction to Pencey Prep's Mr. Holden Caulfield. I recollected one such part from The Catcher in the Rye where Holden determines "certain things, they should stay the way they are." Feeling somewhat emboldened by Holden, I looked around me, tightly rolled the page back into its water-resistant accommodation, secured the cork and launched the bottle back into the ocean. I watched that bottle dance between the moving crests of the waves until it disappeared. I stood for a moment on the edge of some remnant of a rip current and then turned back to continue to help Johnny and all these little kids he had now enlisted as subcontractors for his shaping of his seaside fortress.

Foos yer doos? (How are you?)

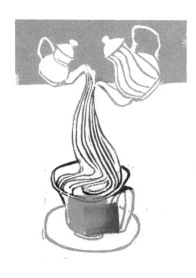

The blare of the commuter train horn on its Saturday schedule precisely every one hour and forty nine minutes was the only major event in our quiescent little hamlet that humdrum morning. Beyond the typical procrastinating of household chores on my day off, I was left alone and prosaic while the rest of my family was scurrying about to a schedule that included stops at a doctor's appointment, field hockey practice and the mall. It wasn't the type of start to the day to begin playing some sort of a culinary adventure like a chef de cuisine like my friend Jared in my own kitchen. I had better opt for a visit to the deli or cafe down in the center of our bucolic town to seek out some sustenance.

I passed the deli and spied far too many townies in their Silverados and F150s in the parking lot fresh from their late evening/early morning big-game hunting of Bambi's mother. My brother-in-law raced by me in his charcoal Toyota Tundra doing a speed in excess of five miles per hour over the posted tortoise limit. I said a quick prayer hoping that the sheriff's deputy I had just seen was preoccupied with his Kill Shot Bravo game app or scrolling through some of the recently divorced local talent on Tinder to notice his "speed". The last thing he needed in his weekend was an upcoming date in front of the town judge. I'd see him later to find out if he dodged the deputy, so I didn't bother to text him at that point.

As I passed town hall on my left, I spun my steering wheel to the right before the railroad tracks and headed down the road running parallel to the station. The "downtown" area is far from the epicenter of economic development – there's the Chinese takeout and a natural healing something or other storefront in what looks like it could have been a general store from a hundred years ago, a stand-alone structure that does some type of high-end artisan restoration of haughty picture frames, a small unassuming bodega that I don't think I have ever stepped foot in, our town post office, which seems to be closed for lunch anytime, I'm in need of mailing something (or checking our post office box), a fine art gallery that seems like it would be in the perfect setting if it weren't completely overlooked by our entire bedroom community, and last but not least, my early meal destination – the cafe.

You may have asked yourself why it is caffe instead of café. I simply don't know and haven't mustered up enough interest to inquire as to the origins of this peculiarity. I parked my truck in the usual spot in front of the post office. While I was gathering my iPhone and personal effects and before leaving my vehicle, I saw this very smartly dressed senior-aged couple leaving the post office.

They were both dressed in that itchy, stodgy estate tweed that reminded me of some well-aged college professor or some gentry in Scotland. He held the door for her as they exited the post office and then quickly readjusted his brown newsboy cap. The timing of our intersection on the sidewalk seemed somewhat oddly cosmically prearranged. I originally wanted to overlook them as I had my objective clearly set on obtaining a grilled breakfast panini from the cafe when I overheard the highlander country woman state to her handsome husband, "He'd be perfect for the job. He's a canny lad."

I pretended to ignore them for a moment but my Catholic guilt and good social graces got the better of me. I turned to them, smiled, and said good morning.

The diminutive woman then asked "Foos yer doos? Can we have a craik laddie?"

Thanks to my UK-based colleagues and having recently returned from a business trip to Ireland that took me to Shannon and Cork, I knew they were asking how I was and they meant that they wished to have a chat.

The perfectly put together older gentleman then shared a brief background that they had a "clarty" bastard that had been performing the work but they had no other options at current – no one and nowhere to turn for help. This issue didn't seem like a typical scam like those emails from Somalia or Botswana so I continued to listen to these two otherwise innocent and quite lovely little couple. While I was listening to them, I began to feel some hunger pangs and heard my stomach start to offer some color commentary to his play-by-play. I abruptly interrupted and asked what precisely was the task at hand.

Gathering himself, the gentleman looked at me and confidently said, "Laddie, it is two jobs actually, we desperately need a pimpmaker and a knocker up."

Without hesitation, they both now continued to ramble on to each other about their recent experiences when I interrupted for a second time and asked what in all of God's creation were they talking about. Apparently, a pimp was a bundle of firewood. The couple had a number of trees cut down on their property and thus needed a pimpmaker. For this first task, they needed a reliable person who could help bundle the wood for them and to potentially sell. I was somewhat but knew I wasn't qualified (or interested) in the first task at hand. I offered the name of the best landscaper in our area – my wife's cousin Eddie. While I'm not sure his wife would embrace the idea of his potential new title, I knew he was the superman that could come to their rescue in their time of need for "pimping."

There was still the other role of the "knocker up" that still desperately required some much needed definition and clarification. While I admit, I did blush a little when I asked about the role and responsibilities of the knocker-up, they did nothing to ease my anxiety.

The woman offered a bit more, she shared that the alternative name of the role saying it was also called a knocker-upper. I shuddered to think where we were headed next down this rabbit hole. Apparently, with their advancing age, they were on several medications and some of these caused them to sleep. Their excessive daytime sleep often made them miss some of their other daily doses of medications and they were in need of knocker-upper, which I was soothed to find out was simply someone who would ensure they would wake up and in this case, help them take their prescription regimen at the required interval.

Blue before sunrise

While there aren't two cats in the yard, "our house is a very, very, very fine house" as the lyrics of Crosby, Stills & Nash profess. In the rustic oasis that are the converted meadows and horse farms stand behemoths enshrouded in beige and gray plastic. Are these domiciles an unspoken testimonial to conformity or simply a tragedy of the tragically white, Christian, Republican, largely upper middle class inhabitants and their lack of creativity? The answer to that question may require some degree of work from the analytics and polling teams at Marist or Quinnipiac. This issue will most unfortunately have to go unanswered for now. Perhaps the more timely (and much bigger) question for our family, friends and neighbors (and the occasional visitor) is the clear non-conformist to this color scheme in our neighborhood that catches their attention and threatens the comforting reality of sameness.

Everyone, I mean everyone know this house. They know the house as people from The Bronx know the Garabedian house on Pelham Parkway – the house that draws thousands of visitors during the Christmas holiday. No, this place isn't another "Christmas house".

It is bright.

It is blue.

At the end of the mountain road as it intersects with the county route, it sits as the fulfillment of someone's pomposity in their pied-à-terre – yes, a bright blue house.

It may not have been the object of such talk in a place like New Orleans or San Francisco but in our town this was an iconic incongruity in the idyllic whistle-stop. While everyone spoke about and clearly knew the house, the overwhelming majority did not know of its inhabitants.

Who lives there?

If you are looking at the front of this blue house from the roadway, the mailbox offers a comforting head tilt to the left. As I had learned in a class on body language and deception two decades ago, the tilting of the head sideways can be a sign of interest, which may be in what is said or happening. It can also be a flirting signal saying, "I am interested in you!". Now, I know what you are thinking, let's not go and start giving human characteristics to inanimate objects. I agree with your view and promise not to anthropomorphize any further. It has been said the greater the tilt, the greater the uncertainty, or the greater the intent to send this type of signal.

Whether you are curious or uncertain (or both) about this bright blue house at this point is still largely irrelevant. It is isn't about you sitting in judgement in your beige or gray home. The hard fact here is this dwelling draws the deliberation of the many homebodies of this town. New and lifelong inhabitants as well as the very old to the very young are a bit bewildered by the blue.

Who lives there, anyway?

On the left side of the overgrown path to the door is a disjointed and misplaced black wrought iron handrail that seems too short for even a small child. Where you would imagine the storybook white picket fence near the curbside on the right side of path is what appears to be some plumber's remnants of some pipe and random fittings pieced together. It would indeed be quite "fitting" if the homeowner was growing some tomatoes and had a hope of securing the vines like Grandpa did in the asphalt jungle on Dalton Road but as a fence in a front yard it was an especial peculiarity among the overgrowth of weeds.

The path diverges immediately from the curbside. The straight path leads to the front door and the left path to an inaccessible small porch with a broken step that is surrounded by wrought iron.

I'll tell you who lives there.

I've seen a man on the small porch on occasion leaning on the artful white pillar that holds up the roof. He's an older man about 80 years of age. He is of slight build, clearly riddled with arthritis, with not much white and silver hair left hair on his head. As best as I can recall his drooping eyes have always appeared somewhat watery, and he has a sad, weathered face that tells the tale of a wearisome life journey.

The time I saw him that I remember most he had a well-worn (what was previously white, now yellowed and sweat stained) v-neck undershirt, khaki-colored shorts (that were clearly made from what was previously a pair of pants), white socks that came up to his knees (like that of University of Maryland basketball standout Walt Williams), and a pair of standard Army issue black combat tropical boots. He's been describe in the same "uniform" every time anyone has seen him and as far as my investigative reporting has surmised.

The very few in town that have engaged him have nicknamed and referenced him as "Crazy Joe". I have heard others call him "Joe the Boxer" claiming he had been a Golden Gloves boxer in his youth. Some others around the town profess he was just punch drunk from too many fights while he was in military service in the South Pacific or Korea or both.

There's a rumor that was overheard one night at Healy's that he was a veteran of both wars and after serving over twenty years in the military "Joe" retired with his college love to the town. As the story has been handed down, some time after losing their infant son to a rare childhood disease shortly after birth, his wife was diagnosed with inoperable primary CNS lymphoma and died within 18 months of their son. Already suffering through and reliving their deaths on a daily basis and wrestling with the flashbacks, nightmares and severe anxiety of post-traumatic stress disorder from his years of military service, Joe became reclusive. He only accepted infrequent visits from a retired priest who was a former military chaplain who had taken residence in the local parish house and from a member from the local VFW who delivered him some groceries, and the occasional hot meal once a week.

One night, about four months after his wife's burial, Joe was battling the jarring and tragic experience of her loss. It was about early evening and the sun had not fully set. His heart and mind was filled with feelings of sadness, anxiety, and he was reliving his recent past shared with the two loves of life. The guilt of not being able to prevent their death from having occurred and his deep feelings of sadness turned to rage. That rage quickly turned into action and "Crazy Joe" decided it is was time to memorialize their passing.

You see, blue was his Annie's favorite color.

Bright blue, not baby blue, was the color Annie wanted for their baby boy's nursery.

As the legend goes (and has clearly been embellished), Joe kicked open the pantry door and jumped down the three short steps into the garage. He rustled through the cans of paint and brushes he had set aside nearly two years earlier. He brought them to the front of the house with his two-story ladder and began to slather the bright blue paint from the dormer windows in the roof structure to the base of the foundation and around the doorway of his domicile.

It was nearly sunrise when he had completed his work and when he was done he sat down on the step of the path leading to the front door and wrote down a few words from the lyrics he remembered from a blues song he had heard – "There is no use looking or ever hoping, or ever hoping to get me back." He taped the paper to the window of his door and finally succumbed to the mental and physical exhaustion – falling asleep on the cool bluestone path that was now speckled in bright blue paint drops.

An Aruban avocation

A harrowing sound lacerates the air and makes for a near cataclysmic cacophony with each thunderous wave that pulverizes the rocks in Noord on the temperate island of Aruba. Day or night, the playlist seems to be on a continuous shuffle but repeating the all-too familiar rhythm of the sea. The green from the near perfectly maintained (what I would assume is Tiff 419 Bermuda Turf) grass and the unmistakable elegance of the California Lighthouse are the only visual breaks amidst the cacti and brittle brush in this singed brown desert landscape that makes up this masterfully designed golf oasis. On this nearly barren Northwest point of land, the makeshift rock formations are only outmatched in arrangement by the impeccable estate homes, multi-bedroom villas and well-appointed condominiums that offer both opulence and clandestineness. For the first time in our nearly two decades of visiting our "One Happy Island" retreat, we left behind our part-time paradise in the pillowy sand of Palm Beach's high rise hotels for a different, more affluent experience.

There was reason for a change in our normal accommodations as well as cause for celebration – we were enjoying both our daughter's high school graduation as well as our cousins' 10th wedding anniversary, and the renewal of their wedding vows. For all the years we have all been traveling here, we had only seen them once, by accident in the airport and heading in an opposing direction. We lucked out that day as we were the ones just arriving!

One very considerate thought from these extended "honeymooners" that must be mentioned was that they had set their renewals well in advance to ensure that anyone that wished, could join them. They wanted to repeat their nuptials with everyone on the island where they had made so many great memories. I had looked forward to this event for well over a year and was so happy to be back on my island of solace.

The flight and airport transfers were completely uneventful except for seeing some celebrity chefs from the Food Network that were traveling to the Aruba Wine, Food & Art Festival. Speaking of uneventful, with an average daytime temperature of 82° Fahrenheit (27° Celsius) and the constant flow of the trade winds, there is something to be said about the predictability of weather for the local meteorologist. That has to be one of the most boring jobs in the world! After our direct flight across the Caribbean from New York and traveling through town, we finally arrived in Noord and at the rugged and picturesque 600 acre community. It was late in the day and we all had only two things on our minds – the pool and our first dinner destination an overdue return to the monumental courtyard dining at Quinta Del Carmen.

A familiar flamenco guitar sound permeated throughout the property as we walked to our Allamanda estate home, and we quickly recognized the familiar tune by Ottmar Liebert from our years of living in Arizona. It seemed every resort or new home community in and around Oranjestad (as in Scottsdale) embraced "Passing Storm" as a part of their not so unique musical branding.

The song was comforting as we proceeded towards our vacation rental with our small bedouin tribe. We were traveling with ten people so the four bedrooms and our own private pool were certainly exactly what the doctor ordered. As we approached the property I recognized what appeared to be a coat of arms – a modified version of the royal standards I had known for the Dutch Royal Family was secured to the door post and a man not much older than myself was relaxing outside. As we proceeded closer to the edifice, and to the man, four armed members of what appeared to be a well-trained security service seemingly appeared out of nowhere. Instead of reacting to this, I was fixated on the subtle change to the standard I had grown so accustomed to seeing with that of Queen Beatrix (and Queen Juliana).

The rosette was missing.

The rosette in the ribbon of the Military Order of William had been replaced by a bow. This item was the royal standard of the second youngest monarch in Europe after Felipe VI of Spain. Our traveling circus were all now looking at the man sitting in the chair – we were in the presence of royalty on our doorstep, King Willem-Alexander of the Netherlands. He had recently ascended to the throne in 2013 when his mother Queen Beatrix abdicated after her reign of exactly 33 years.

It was definitely one of those moments when you look back and think that it lasted for 20 minutes when it was only maybe two.

One of the members of the security service was asking me questions but I didn't hear a word he said. I was clicking through in my mind all the answers in the Jeopardy category on the House of Orange-Nassau and running a parallel track about royal etiquette –

- Should my wife and daughters curtsey?
- Should I bow or genuflect?
- Should I address him as "Your Royal Highness"?

For a moment, I felt (and probably looked like) Clark W. Griswold and his family in European Vacation. I came fast forward out of my dream sequence and back to reality blurting out – "Your Majesty, we just arrived from your Mom's airport."

I could feel our entire family turn and stare at me with completely puzzled looks on their faces. The King turned away and laughed to himself as the security service motioned to us to continue walking down the path. One of them mumbled under their breath something about not knowing how to behave in front of royalty but I was still in a state of shock that the King was staying in what was clearly our vacation home.

Where were we going to stay? When was His Royal Highness going to be checking out?

Never mind those details, why were we now just walking down this path?

As one of the King's Netherlands ninjas promptly explained, they needed the four bedroom Allamanda estate home for the King for some security reasons and we were switched to stay at the five bedroom Allamanda estate home. We had not been on the island for two hours and we literally received a royal upgrade – wait until the rest of the family and our own royal couple hear about this!

While we told our tale at dinner, we wondered if he was on vacation with his family or tending to some governmental affairs. Later that evening, we returned to our vacation home to find a note affixed to our door. The envelope and letterhead bore the seal of the King. It was an invitation for our family to a gala reception – an exquisite five-course menu by some of the island's top chefs during the Aruba Wine, Food & Art Festival. The royal treatment would continue for this trip!

A mimical finesse?

The district of Dalston originally began as a hamlet in the parish of Hackney in the northeast part of London. The origins of its name was unremarkable as it developed on either side of Dalston Lane. While I was standing approximately 4,624 miles away from Dalston in New Orleans, Louisiana, I couldn't help but think of the wall art I had seen there. You know the one I am referring to.

You have seen it replicated on those bootleg t-shirts on sale at the flea markets. On my last visit to New York City, I spied some wannabe rapper teenagers walking around dressed like it. The wall art I'm referring was created by Banksy – the image of the old school hip hop dressed kid wearing the backwards hat, a long gold chain with what appears to be some type of gun charm, while holding a boombox in his left hand and a teddy bear in his right hand.

Yes, you read that correctly, a teddy bear.

Was this a stunt of some kind?

Was this kid a street performer?

Maybe he was also a fan of Banksy?

Standing next to a lamppost down Pirate's Alley in New Orleans was the old school hip hop Banksy kid's doppelgänger. I checked out his gear as if I was checking off a Costco shopping list. The kid was wearing the backwards hat – check. He's got a long gold chain with what appears to be some type of New Orleans Saints old gold "fleur-de-lis" charm – appropriate for our geographic setting. He was holding a boombox in his left hand and there it was, the teddy bear in his right hand. There was something different though, besides the easily identifiable Saints icon. A few inches away from him appeared to be some kind of bucket or pottery.

Street performers in New Orleans come in all shapes and sizes. Many have all sorts of gimmicks. I'm not referring to beads and those type of shenanigans – I'm talking street scams. The one I laugh at every time I visit the French Quarter is when I'm approached and told – "Bet I can tell ya where you got your shoes." This kid had to have something going on like that.

The lamppost he was next to was only slightly off to the left of center a few yards down on this atramentous and soggy cobblestone street. These rounded river rocks were the exact kind used to pave the streets of N'awlins a very long time ago. They aren't particular comfortable on your feet when walking across them and certainly standing on the rounded cobbles for even a few minutes can be painful. In spite of any podiatric paroxysm, this stoic non-sound blasting sentinel stood stable. As I approached nearer to him, he didn't flinch. Before I could reach him, a few frat boys walked past and one pulled up for a make believe fade away jump shot and launched a few coins into the hip hop kid's bucket.

I picked up my pace as I wanted to get quickly past the clearly inebriated Greek-lettered Lords of the Flies. The predictable machismo pushing match with the "hooligan" brothers followed as they proceeded down the street away from me. I reached the breathing Banksy analogue and admired his serenity as he simply stood there in his hip hop poise.

He didn't blink.

He didn't even gesticulate towards me.

Now kneeling down on one knee to see what was written on his bucket, I realized it was more of a refined redware earthenware clay pot from colonial times, the kind you see on the Antiques Roadshow on PBS. Inscribed on the exterior with was clearly a Sharpie 44001 Magnum permanent markers, was the word "HUNNY" in all capital letters. The only difference was the letter N in the middle was turned backwards like

Winnie the Pooh's hunny pot. I reached in the pocket of my jeans and threw all the change I had into this Nawlins Banksy's bank.

As I did, I whispered in my best southern drawl, "Yo, Banksy hip hop kid, betcha I can tell ya where you got your shoes."

This picket of Pirate's Alley proceeded to break his composure and yell out "You got 'dem shoes on your feet" while he hit play on his boombox to Mac Miller's "Nikes On My Feet." The irony is that particular video starts with Mac walking down a dark street near some lampposts.

Art imitating life? You decide.

I call it ironic ingenuity.

A galactic glimmer

The crew had traveled some 40 light years to reach this distinct set of five planets. The planets were surrounding the sun-like star they had admired since their time as amateur astronomers in their childhood. There was the one planet deemed "super-earth" and four other gas giants, one of which possessed a habitable zone and has temperatures similar to earth. This object was no ordinary star and these were no ordinary astronauts.

The star is quite visible to the naked eye in our own night sky from Earth, situated in the dimmest of all of the constellations – Cancer. These intrepid explorers bore the somewhat predictable insignia of the "crab" on their arm patches and either in some twist of fate or some not-so-private administrative joke they "coincidentally" each shared a birthday between June 22nd and July 22nd.

Like all good people born under the sign of Cancer, the team had grown very attached to one another. There were five crew members, all with extensive military training, each selected for their distinct set of skills:

- Commander Tom "Cappy" Miller, a tenacious and highly imaginative team leader, he was charged with overall mission success and the safety of crew as they set to explore this bold new planet
- Pilot Matilda "Fly Girl" Ryan, a bit more sympathetic and silent type who was responsible for the obvious operating of the shuttle and deploying the use unmanned vehicles plus an additional responsibility for the on-planet science experiments

- Mission Specialist Tom "No Nicknames" Horvath, the pessimistic and pointed engineering lead in coordinating system operations
- Mission Specialist Dr. Barry "Doc Jack" Jackson, the highly persuasive physician focused on crew health, activity planning and use of consumable resources on board for the duration of the space flight and on planet
- Payload Specialist Edward "Smarts" Reiben, the deeply intuitive and somewhat insecure scientist that was already carrying out many of the experimental tests on the various payload (cargo)

These space sailors or star fliers had shown intense endurance and stamina coming the longest way any humans had ever traveled in space. Their reward would be to be the first to step foot on a planet twice the size of earth that maintained a surface that past rovers had determined was covered in graphite and up to one-third was covered in diamonds. As much as Horvath wasn't too convinced that he required a nickname, he was even less convinced of the idea that diamonds lined the surface, citing the planet as the "rhinestone cowboy" planet. This situation wasn't this crew's first rodeo together and several had worked closely together on other missions. The core group here had known each other for over 16 years and were loyal and sympathetic to each other to an extreme. Fly Girl and Smarts were still the new kids on this crew and they had experienced flight training, survival training and basic mission testing at Johnson Space Center together in Texas.

As they approached this "super-earth" planet 55 Cancri e, the shuttle monitors assessed the surface temperature at well past 3900 degrees Fahrenheit. As Doc Jack daydreamed of his island retirement home off the coast of South Florida that was awaiting him back on our Earth, he had recollected that at the press conference at Yale where the researchers had noted that the planet was likely "unusually dense". He continued to wonder what they had meant by this as he took a small bite into his "dense" slice of his birthday cake the crew had surprised him with the night prior.

Cappy and Fly Girl were at the controls bringing the shuttle near to the surface for landing when surface lifescan monitors began to go off the charts. Cappy at first thought it had been just an electromagnetic field issue and quickly dismissed the warning. The soft landing was the signature move for Fly Girl and some claimed she was more rough in putting butter on toast.

The crew were preparing to disembark as they heard a loud rumbling. The disconcerting reverberation resembled a rolling thunder but had a distinctive, more thumping or pounding-type tone to it. As Horvath opened the shuttle doors for the rest of the crew, Cappy led the way for the team, donning the first suit capable of protecting human life in such extreme heat. He was unanimously chosen to be the first to take this next "giant leap". As the first to exit, he was the first to see and confirm that the surface was indeed, this mysterious graphite and yes, dazzling diamond combination but that wasn't the only amazing initial sight for the crew.

They were greeted this day, June 29, by diamond studded rocky creatures partially resembling the giant rock characters depicted in Darren Aronofsky's Noah that Russell Crowe starred in back in 2014. While there are no actual giant rock creatures illustrated in the written biblical account of Noah, Genesis 6:1–4 does tell the readers of the Nephilim. The term which means "fallen ones" when translated into English, the Nephilim were the product of copulation between the divine beings and human women. The book goes on to describe that "The Nephilim were on earth in those days – and also afterward." Were these strange rock giant inhabitants of the planet 55 Cancri e actually the Nephilim?

They at first appeared far more humanoid and nimble as if the Marvel Comics' Fantastic Four rock solid character "The Thing" – Benjamin "Ben" Grimm. Were they the fallen angels described as "The Watchers" we read about in the Book of Enoch (an apocryphal collection of texts, the earliest dating to the third century B.C.E.)?

Cappy and the intrepid "Crab" crew of shuttle mission 2744 landing on what was now confirmed by Horvath as "clearly not the rhinestone cowboy planet" was just at the beginning of their adventure of exploration. Their first goal was to uncover how to communicate to these inhabitants and establish their shared values as a compass to guide their interactions and next steps together – this response would be critical to their mission success.

The golden experience

The artist for the travel guide had illustrated some of the mix of deciduous and coniferous trees we would encounter along the meandering trail but I was certain I could sketch those better from memory. This place wasn't a hike by any hiking definition – this event was an effortless walk. The paved loop trail was short and easy just like the attention span of most of the out-of-shape and not-so-intrepid tourists. I recall my first visit with my brother Benjamin when he was nine, and now, a decade later, we were here together again with some of his soccer teammates from college.

Benji had already commented several times to me why we were wasting our time on this trail. "We could rent motorized wheelchairs and experience this like the blue-hairs over here," he said to me about four seconds out of our rented Rav4. "We won the damn lottery Alex, it is time to go big or go back to the lodge."

He was right.

We did win the lottery.

Well, not that lottery, but the one that made this trip matter to us more than any vacation before.

You see, one way to be allowed on the premier route in Yosemite and to get to hike to the top of the most iconic granite dome in the continental United States is to win a preseason lottery with an application in March. It was now July and my little brother was not feeling as nostalgic as I was. Sure, I was ecstatic about the permit and that we were finally going to do Half Dome together, but some of my fondest memories were here. Experiencing the park once again through a rekindling of our first hike on the Lower Yosemite Fall Trail was precisely the best way to kick off our adventure – especially with our guests.

Scrambling off any of the trails will ultimately lead to injury for most hikers. Of course, we were going off the trail to "see what we could see" as my brother so aptly put it. He was laughing in that mischievous way that brothers laugh when they have an idea and you know you are heading down a slippery slope with him! In this case, that slippery slope came twofold – first in his thinking and second, well, we'd been here before and knew that above the wooden footbridge that crosses Yosemite Creek that the rocks and boulders are slippery even when they are technically dry. We found that out the hard way when I introduced my left shin to a jagged edge of one of the residential rocks on our last trip.

We were well off the trail with our courageous and mildly contemptuous chieftain leading the way as we headed to Lower Yosemite Fall. The water is peak at this time of year so we were in for a truly stunning view of the falls in their omnitude. The "normal" hike was roughly about a mile when you stay to the trail – we were already well over a mile off track with my brother's mental compass charting the course but I didn't mind. He was a few steps ahead of me when I saw him stop and stoop down. We had stumbled upon a nest and it was unlike anything we had seen before.

Our elevation was hovering around 4,000 feet and I wasn't certain what kind of bird or reptile could build a nest this close to such a high volume trail. It wasn't the safest of real estate for a "growing" family of wildlife. There were a ton of deer and other fauna nearly omnipresent by the trails awaiting the generosity of the "rugged" city slickers donning all their well-coordinated outdoor swag to truly feel the momentum for that braggadocious woodland selfie.

I asked Benji to describe what he was because I couldn't peer around the now huddled mass of his soccer mates and their backpacks. "Alex, it is a bunch of, well, gold eggs," he exclaimed.

Gold eggs? What the what?!?

As I genuflected to also have a closer look, dodging their massively over packed gear for such a short hike, I saw he was telling the truth. At that moment, one of the golden eggs started to hatch as I was rifling through my Google search app looking for pictures of gold eggs and indigenous birds to California. It was one of the quietest moments I had ever experienced. We were witnessing the miracle of life and we were all waiting what would happen next with each passing second.

We were witnessing each fracture, and the struggle to escape of the tiny creature trapped safely inside. We didn't want to take our eyes off of the golden shell, speak a word or even breathe! As the final breech was made, we could see that this poult was more than small when he was finally hatched. If I had to guess it may be only weighed a few ounces at best – what a tiny little bird! For such a petite fellow, he was quite eager to let the world know of his arrival and I wondered still what kind of bird he was and also where was his Mom. I was sure at that point she may have heard his arrival and was lurking close to where we were hovering over her nest.

I looked down at the remaining golden eggs, and our new found not so feathered friend and wondered still about his species. Scores of images were now populated in my phone and I quickly surmised this young fellow was a Rio Grande Wild Turkey (Meleagris gallopavo intermedia). It all made sense to me now – these turkeys inhabit brush areas near streams and rivers or mesquite, pine and scrub oak forests. As I was scanning the details of the write-up, I realized that they can be found up to 6,000 feet elevation. I still disagreed with the real estate selection as it was far too open of an area for predators (or people) to disrupt their "humble home."

As I read on, it made even more sense to me as these wild turkeys favor areas that are more open than the wooded habitat favored by the ones in our backyard in Connecticut. I could tell the guys were already

well-past the point of waiting around for the next reverential parturition so I looked at my compass, parting the way between them and said "Time to get to the base of the Lower Falls boys." We'd get back on track and hopefully back on the trail. Benji's temporary off-trail detour provided us all with a "golden opportunity" to go through a blessed event we had not shared together and it was the first of many more memories that would be made.

A routine predicament

Today is my 2,569th day of retirement. It still feels a bit surreal. Yes, I am proud to say it does get better with time. I am the master of my domain and my schedule, though my schedule has been all too predictable for most of the past seven years. On most mornings like today, without the kids, I'm up checking social media, and the various family chat threads and then I'm out. Not out as in back to sleep, I'm out on the town for the day.

My destination for the duration is my park bench – more about that in a bit. It is a partly cloudy morning with temperatures expected to rise to 79 degrees later in the day. I used to take my hooptie on my morning forty weight run but since I've retired, I'm sporting the velocipede. I don't mind the two wheeler especially in my suburban area getting to navigate the rail trails and byways around the reservoir system.

Coming out of my fortress of solitude on the lake (which is really the reservoir and not an actual lake), I make a quick left onto the portentous Route 100 (which has a double identity as Stoneleigh Avenue). I pass between the hospital center on my right and the barns on my left. Passing the Drewville intersection, the signage makes you feel as if you can reach any destination by going east or west but that going north, well, not so much as that is a return to civilization. Immediately passing the intersection, the roadway becomes enshrouded by trees. Both the town and the county have extolled the importance of trees, specifically defining the way trees help in "preventing soil erosion and flooding, absorb air pollution, provide oxygen, yield advantageous micro-climatic effects, have an intrinsic aesthetic quality, offer a natural barrier to noise and provide a natural habitat for the wildlife." When the wind is still like this morning, the trees appear to be nothing more than wooden mannequins well-dressed in the latest greens and browns for some sensational seasonal showcase.

With the posted speed limit topping out at 45 miles per hour and no dedicated bike lane, I have often wondered the risk-benefit of this stretch of road. With parts of the reservoir now on either side of me, I approach Hughson Road for decision time. Do I continue straight, which would cut my time (and scenery) significantly to my bench or navigate the serpentine asphalt adventure that is Hughson? As I make the right turn and wind around the twists and turns, the scenery shifts somewhat and it feels like I have been transported to Dagobah (no offense Master Yoda). I quickly pass all the residential homes, condos, and Lakeview and Kelly roads with little effort. There's the Restoration Hardware office (or is it a mini-distribution center), the coal and wood pellet place and the pool and spa store I would frequent if I had a pool or spa. I finally get to the rail trail – it is my typical backdoor route to my park bench to avoid the vehicular traffic but something is motivating me today to take the long view drive this early morn.

Continuing to pedal on past the plumbing supply, I see that their lot is already filled with their regular group of contractors and plumbers. That's one business that's success is always going down the drain – true story, true story.

I speed up a bit and make it past the vacated store front formerly known as the Tilly Foster General Store.

In all my years living in town and raising my own family here, I just haven't stepped foot in the place or that Morning Star Trading Company (just past Root Avenue). You know the place, they have the moccasins and Mexican blankets that are outside for sale year round. I'm surprised some of the local delinquents haven't stolen the entire inventory as a prank (at least, I have never heard or read about it).

I make the turn left and begin the grind uphill on Route 6. As I reach the top, my internal battery acid meter is on flat-line. I put my head down, shift gears and picture my park bench and a handful of varnish remover to fill my AM quota. I literally don't even look up until I make the right turn into Put Plaza and there she was with the welcoming look on her face. My twin-tailed mysterious mermaid singing her siren song – calling out to all her caffeine fiends. It is here where you will find me for the duration on my park bench.

If Starbucks in my town were Cheers, I'd have a leading role at best. At worst, I'd be a most memorable character actor, but looking a bit like DeNiro, they would never get out of line. There are some days that I think that it is something about the rubenesque icon that mesmerizes and hypnotizes each of us because we have all certainly had better cups of joe.

I give the nod to the barista – she knows.

I need not say a word.

They script my name today – fancy, huh?

They fill my cup (as a member, I'll get the refill thing going in a few minutes after I upload this one) and then it happens.

Time stops.

No, not my watch.

All the time grinds to a halt.

Nothing is moving, not a "creature was stirring" except me.

No more of that definitive sound of Sonny Rollins' jazz tenor sax on the acclaimed "St. Thomas" tune.

There is silence from that godforsaken milk frother.

I look around as if I were in a "Twilight Zone" episode – you can imagine the scene from a movie where the main character then breaks the fourth wall as if in "Ferris Bueller" or the more recent "Deadpool".

That's me but at this point, there's no one to turn to.

I'm now going through the regular salutations of the morning like the cordialities Will Smith's character Dr. Robert Neville in "I Am Legend" communicates in the video store scene. I take my perch on my park bench to take it all in with my heavenly hot stuff handily in my grips.

As I peer around, I noticed one of the young ladies is sporting what appears to be an engagement ring. She's a regular, her now fiance is more infrequent. I believe she is a freelance medical writer and her now husband to be is a hospitalist or in hospitality up at the medical center.

I can't recollect which.

I give her the nod of acknowledgement, tip my navy cap with those easily identifiable interlocking white letters of N and Y and say "God bless" before taking my next sip.

Don't get me wrong, this is all just settling in for me and still nothing is moving in my coffee klatsch. It is a most unusual circumstance – but not concerning me in the slightest, at least not yet. It could get a little weird if these people don't start to breathe or drink their lattes. I check my pulse to know that I'm not dead like some of these fellow fine patrons. I'm all good. The pulse is right where it should be for a Friday.

Have you ever had that one moment where you are checking off everything you have either just done or were about to do? It wasn't until I arrived at the airport to head out on vacation that I realized I forgot my swimsuit. This event was that kind of moment for me. I reviewed the events leading up to this very second and still I just couldn't place the trigger to this whole cascade of calmness.

Then, it hit me.

Rush.

No, I wasn't in a rush and these fine frozen friends and neighbors were certainly not going anywhere! When the barista handed me my brewed prescription for caffeine withdrawal, she wrote "Rush" instead of "Russ". That is exactly when time stopped in this contrapositive coffee conundrum!

Rush? Was that a sign or something?

What caused my entire world to literally come to a halt?

It was at that moment I felt my body twitch as if in a hypnic jerk. You know that involuntary twitch which occurs just as a person is beginning to fall asleep. It makes me wake up suddenly…wait a second. Was I coming out of some sort of dream sequence?

I awoke in the coffee shop with my cousin tapping me on the shoulder. She was asking me if I were okay. I said to her "I've been rushing around the last few days and must have needed this even more than I thought." I looked around to see the usual motley crew in their regular seats and yes, I was on my "park bench" but I had fallen to sleep.

I looked down at my cup and there was my name in script and it was spelled incorrectly "Rush". My unfinished reply to the text message from my cousin read…

"Meet at the park bench? Don't rush."

Clouds far behind me

The tornado notifications started coming across each of our mobile devices. We were under full alert that something was about to happen between a drizzle and full on armageddon. It was the end of the month and the end of the quarter so many of us were unable leave the office early for the extended holiday weekend. The caliginous sky became extremely unpropitious. Between the resounding thunder and the velocious lightning, we were distracted from our work to awe in Mother Nature's seasonal flash of irreparable fury. The insufferable crashing of the clouds together boldly hinted that the show was just about to begin.

From our fifth floor perch, we have 180 degree views above the tree line and in our corner office the view expands to 270 degrees. Our colleagues have a ringside seat for literally every storm raging across the sound shore or through the Hudson Valley. This one was different. The alerts said tornado and this event would be a first for all of us who had shared so many epic storms together in the past.

The winds picked up their acceleration and agitation as the mighty oaks and maples thrashed wildly against the evergreen giants that surrounded the perimeter of the building. The rain surged at an inconceivable rate like several car wash sprayers on hyper speed. The force of all of these elements coming together all at once and so quickly terrorized our remaining staff. It was unanimous that no one was going to take the risk in the current storm and leave the premises before the end of this ferocity.

"Look at that, over there, over your shoulder," exclaimed Mark. As I turned around to see what he was referring to, I was blinded and a bit stunned by the brightness of the western setting sun amidst the darkness. The murkiness of the tornado-threatening sky had subsided rather quickly as the white sunlit rays stepped into a more prominent feature role alongside some of the other celestial bodies, reflecting its majesty in every rain droplet that continued to trickle down across the county.

As if it was written in a storybook, the most audacious and illuminating, perfectly full-arched rainbow now presented before our eyes. The heavenly reward of red colored light exclaimed its presence at its anointed 42 degrees – bending and being the most accommodating as it hugged its sisterly spectrum. Orange and yellow collaborating only ever so slightly less together. Blue and violet shifting downward in the tightest configuration – bending the least in their uncompromising lower ranked positions.

It was in this moment that I realized where the end of the rainbow (at least metaphorically) may be. While Judy Garland, Israel "Iz" Kamakawiwo'ole and countless crooners have dared to ask in their lyrics "Beyond the rainbow why, oh, why can't I?" It wasn't about going beyond the rainbow – it was going in.

The answer I propose of where the end of the rainbow might be right, could be where we begin again. As the Josh Groban lyrics to Believe share, "Destinations are where we begin again."

Enjoy each storm.

Be rewarded by the random occasion where light hits the front of the droplet, bends as it enters, reflects back of the droplet and then leaves again through the front, back toward us.

The rainbow is a reflection of our soul's journey and the events that unfold in front of us. The end of the rainbow is a chance to begin again and be that reflection to others that we want to see in our own lives.

A midnight paradox

Is it better to hate to love something or love to hate something?

Is it even a question or is it a consideration between these extremes?

I couldn't stop thinking about this as I wrestled in the sheets and readjusted my pillows. I found myself now and then stopping for a moment and becoming fixated on the sepia tone tapestry of the Mariposa Sequoia Grove hanging on the wall above the headboard on my Pacific Ocean Blue-painted wainscot paneled wall.

What could be the answer to this question that continues to elude me this evening?

To provide you some background, I'm in a unique and charming studio in Palo Alto. Yes, I live in Silicon Valley and I'm an engineer. Yes, I work at a company who's stated mission is to organize the world's info and make it accessible and useful. Yes, you have likely heard about it before and use it on average at least 76 times a day starting from while you are still in bed and until it is the last thing you do before you fall asleep.

My humble dwelling is located in a vibrant and bustling area off of University Avenue. At this time, my landlord is looking for me to pay over $2500/month for my next six month lease. Before you have any sympathy for me, that's cheap around here. I'm steps away from some of the most eclectic dining and shopping on the Peninsula. You may read about and talk about going "green" but I'm the poster child – I've got access to Caltrain and I need not own a car as I have access to a high-tech, low impact employee shuttle to work (they run on 5% biodiesel).

Life is good.

Yes, "Life is good" as the crusher graphic tees and other apparel and accessories casually proclaim. Disclaimer though, I've looked on their site and even the "Life is good" people have a bold reality check. They state the following: "Life is not perfect. Life is not easy. Life is good." You didn't know that did you? Interesting, eh?

That's not the line I see printed on all this swag around town. I may have missed the items in the "Life is not perfect" holiday sale online while having our yearly controlled chaos Christmas dinner at my in-laws.

No, I don't "hate to love" this company, their ever-chill icon, or their lofty ideal of "spreading the power of optimism".

It is ALL good.

You see what I did there?

The company continues to specify that "optimism is not irrational cheerfulness or "blind positivity". It's a pragmatic approach for approaching life."

As an engineer who is trapped in the confines of my bed for the next six to seven hours, I surmise that at least at this point I'm leaning towards the hate to love. In the category of love to hate though, I believe politics (especially presidential candidates), and those bumper stickers (especially those god awful stick figure families) fit perfectly. I also can't forget or forgive former Red Sox pitcher Pedro Martinez for his actions in the 2003 American League Championship Series (and all Red Sox players past and present except Pedroia and Big Papi). In the hate to love, cleaning my apartment is definitely ranking high atop the list of things but it may surprise you to know that it is technology and being constantly connected that ranks way up there as number one.

At this point, you are saying to yourself, sure, a Silicon Valley engineer that hates to love technology and being constantly connected. How believable is that? I come from a town over three hours outside the valley. My hometown of Groveland has a population of 3,388 and sits at an elevation of 2,552′. It is the land where both cellular signals and wifi goes to die and I long for it. If you haven't tried to go off the grid, head out to Stanislaus or Yosemite and you'll have no other choice in the matter.

We still have no telephone and no television and it is just perfect.

This isn't an indictment on technology or being constantly connected. At this point personally and professionally, we all need time to unplug. The second after I wake up every morning my iPhone reminds me of all of the scheduled activities that have been committed to me. Before I rise from these sheets in the next six hours (at this point in my ramblings), I'll have checked my emails and statuses. I'm being honest with myself when I share that I hate to love this most of all and long for the day where I can't connect any longer. I hope to be in a position where I don't need to receive notifications and I can reestablish the true personal connections that were meaningful at a much earlier time in my analogue life. The type of relationship shared over a meal without everyone grabbing for their mobile devices and where stories and jokes were the basis of our engagement with one another instead of asking if you saw or liked my post.

For now, I'll set my alarm on my iPhone and wake up as if I do every morning to Wham's "Wake Me Up Before You Go-Go" and hope these paradoxical thoughts in my mind can quickly pass. The alternative will be to start counting sheep, or the number of joints in the tung and groove wainscot paneling, which are both better options than some artificial ocean sound I could download from iTunes.

A curious attraction

By some accounts, the girl would have been called flighty, by others they would have tagged her most certainly as hugger-mugger at such a young age. Her mother Rylie was the complete contrapositive at that age and certainly now at her advanced age. Rylie was born near a rye field to a tenant farmer, and a coster wife (fruit seller), she was quite conservative and became a hand woman to the wife of a noted physician in London.

As the myth goes, Rylie had seen an early performance of Shakespeare's play 'The Merchant of Venice' where the name Jessica belongs to the daughter of Shylock. Rylie fell in love with the name of the character and convinced her husband in 1596 to bestow it on their second daughter, Jessica Knight. She was a diminutive little lass with blonde locks and hazel eyes. She was the most adored of her siblings by her much older cousins and her entire family was smiling whenever they were around her.

By her fourth birthday, Jessica had become a bit of a fixture at Gilbert House and quite familiar with every nook and cranny. While Rylie tended to the daily needs of Lady Gilbert, Jessica could expand her idiosyncratic curiosities and capacious imagination throughout the home. She was not allowed to play outside and could not disturb the Gilbert's three English Water Spaniels while they were sleeping. The dogs were older with a touch of rheumatism setting in. The trio had seen their fair share of days swimming and diving after ducks during the many hunting excursions by the good doctor.

Recently, Dr. Gilbert had published his masterwork "De Magnete" where he presented a large volume of the results of his research into magnetism and electricity. Serving now as the court physician to Queen Elizabeth, I (and before to King James I), he emerged as one of the most respected and successful physicians in all of England. While "De Magnete" debunked many popular scientific theories at the time, Dr. Gilbert had also become the first person to fully explain the workings of a magnetic compass.

It was an extraordinarily early morning for Rylie and Jessica as the two made their journey across a foggy London town to Gilbert House. The lady of the house was already performing her usual rawgabbit and her husband was at work in his study. Dr. Gilbert was carefully reviewing lecture notes on electricity. He was set to give a lecture at the Royal College of Physicians when the mother-daughter duo arrived.

Jessica was all-too familiar with the protocol of Gilbert House, especially at that time of the morning. While she did have the unchecked use of the entire home throughout the day, when Dr. Gilbert was at home, or in his study, she could not disturb him. She was waiting patiently for him to leave. She sat quietly on the bottom landing step of the staircase playing with her small doll and humming to herself.

Dr. Gilbert always loved having Jessica around but in his haste this morning, he didn't acknowledge her on his way out the door. Jessica heard the door open to his study and seconds later, the front door of Gilbert House slams close. She got up off the stair and slowly crept her way towards his study. As she peeked through the opening, she thought the room was erstwhile, filled with books and rare oddities. It was similar to a layout of wizard's tower room filled with magic and books that she imagined in the bedtime stories her father had shared.

As she entered the room, she saw that all of Dr. Gilbert's papers and various vessels were strewn across the room as if he didn't know how or where to best place them in order. Jessica was too young to recognize the Latin names written out for the contents of the larger vessels –

iron, cobalt, and nickel on some and rare earth elements of cerium, neodymium, samarium, and europium on the others. In addition to the various metals and alloys of transition and rare earth elements, he had an arrangement of calculations, descriptions, and diagrams of metal oxides. As it was her mother's responsibility to help Lady Gilbert, Jessica at first played the role of a fudgel, mimicking the gestures of the way her mother would go about her work but in this case not really doing much of anything.

Her curiosity then turned into alacrity.

Jessica began to organize, or what she thought was organizing, in her puerile mind.

She was resolved to help get this desk clear and the room clean for Dr. Gilbert so that she and her mother may sleep in on the morrow and not set out so early again.

As she began to touch each leather-bound book and move around the vessels she noticed her hand becoming more and more attached to them. She was able to pry her hand off, but the sensation of sticking to each was growing stronger in each of her handling of the various containers.

Jessica became distraught as she could not remove her hand from one of the smaller containers of metal oxide. She thought less about crying out since to cry out would reveal her trespass. Despite her best effort, the magnetism continued to grow stronger in her hands, arms and even her feet. Jessica had somehow attained superhuman abilities and was quickly uncovering how she was able to move some of the vessels toward her and others away from her. It appeared the more she thought about the simple task at hand, the more this newfound ability manifested itself.

After organizing the last bit of papers, Jessica moved towards the door, grabbed the handle and opened the door to the study to walk out. As she grabbed the venerable handle, she pulled it completely through the door.

Now holding the door handle in her left hand and staring mesmerized at the gaping hole in the door, Jessica was first fascinated at the feat of strength.

Her mesmeric state quickly turned to trepidation as she thought of how she would explain this all to her mother, Lady Gilbert and Dr. Gilbert when he arrived back home. This occurrence was all very confusing and her mood quickly became somber considering the irreparable damage she had done. This unfortunate event wouldn't be an easy explanation of what had happened to her or the door.

Word of honor

As a freshman high school soccer player in Mesquite, he was already the varsity equivalent of his fellow Aquarian, Cristiano Ronaldo dos Santos Aveiro. Like Ronaldo, he scored at least one goal in every game he ever played. David Ermenegildo Indolor had become known as "Mr. Futbol" in his youth, playing the forward position and serving as the team captain on every team, at every level. Opposing teams would double- and triple-team him and somehow he still managed to either make an incredible assist to a teammate or break free and score. With his initials "DES" his close friends and teammates would tease him that it was his destiny that he would be a professional soccer player.

While he spent much of his free time following La Liga and his favorite players on the various Spanish clubs, he cherished the memories of those weekends watching the Portugal national team with his avô Antonio above all. David was involved in soccer in every part of his life and he couldn't see a day without chatting about the game he loved or finding time to practice the dynamic moves like the greats.

The next spring, when he turned fifteen, a great tragedy struck the Indolor family. David's mother, who thought she was simply having headaches and symptomatology related to menopause was diagnosed with grade IV astrocytoma. This is the most common and most aggressive cancer that begins in the brain. Within a few short months, in June, Anabela Indolor had passed away. In an angry rage, David swore never to play soccer again.

As a local sports reporter, I had covered some of the stories of David's early successes in high school and could validate firsthand of the now near mythical status of his "scorchers" with both feet. This terrible medical misfortune with his mother and his pledge not to play was something I thought about profiling but I had gotten distracted in some other work and didn't get around to it. I thought it was quite admirable but hoped that after a season hiatus, family and friends would convince David to return to the pitch.

He did not return his sophomore year.

His junior year came and went and David was nowhere close to a soccer ball or a field.

Some point in his rising senior summer, I heard his name bandied about that he was contemplating a return but this idea was simply optimistic rumors from some very uninformed people in the community. The other rumor I heard nearly knocked me out of bed – it was today, literally just a few minutes ago, 9:40 on a Saturday morning in what is now late October.

I had slept in late, and I was going to clearly miss an early local high school football team I wanted to cover.

It was then that I just received a text from a soccer referee that also officiated football that said simply stated, "Mr. Futbol is now playing football – call me later."

I checked my schedule for his undefeated high school football team and saw that today would be their last game before the playoffs started in their division. I knew I needed to get out of bed and would have to rush to get ready to be there across town.

I fumbled with my keys as I darted out the door to the house and hopped into my truck. The thought of David potential kicking a football and it exploding in mid-air made me smile.

What were the circumstances that led him to play football?

What happened to the team's senior kicker that had signed early to play at a noted NCAA Division I program?

My reporter instincts were on overload with questions as I arrived at the field.

I pulled into my usual media parking spot and noticed that the visiting team was taking warm-ups but David's team was not on the field as of yet. I stopped for a second and thought – did I really just label this undefeated team David's team already?

My heart was beating rapidly and my palms were sweaty – either I was having a heart attack at the ripe old age of 44 or the whole situation had me all worked up.

Instead of climbing to my usual early perch in the press box, I decided to hang out by the entrance to the field where the home team enters down from their locker room. It is a rather steep sloping grade and I have often wondered if the contractors were intoxicated that put down the asphalt there. Helmet after helmet descended onto the field, many of them cordially saying good morning and many giving me a high five – these were good boys and they had worked hard all season to be undefeated. I grabbed the special teams coach, and he blurted, "Yeah, it's true" as he summarily dismissed me with a smirk and a quick fix to the brim of his cap.

I looked around the field at Memorial Stadium but there was no kicker warming up at all for the home team. The clock was running down on the pre-game time and the home team made their way back up the hill for their typical grand entrance and senior day announcements. As they filed in one by one, David's name wasn't announced. There was some speculation from the people standing near to me of what injury had happened to the current senior kicker, but I would have hoped to have that clarified in the game notes as I got to the press box.

The home team won the toss and deferred to receive in the second half.

Where was this kid?

The coolness of the autumn breeze danced among the warmth of the partly sunny rays beaming down. I was now wiping my brow as in my haste I had put on far too many layers.

The locker room door was already being held open by a large cobblestone that someone had dug out from the nearby curb.

The scene was like something out of a dream sequence in a campy 80s film – it was literally like all time just stopped.

David stepped out of the locker room appearing in what was clearly the cleanest uniform in the entire county.

He was alone and slowly began to walk what appeared to be towards me but I knew he was headed to the entrance of the field. We locked eyes for a moment and I heard him say through his mouthpiece "Hey Scoop, thanks for coming out this morning."

My eyes could not believe what I was seeing, my ears heard what David had said, but it was like everything was happening in slow motion.

I heard plenty of professional, college and high school athletes talk about how the game slows down, but I had never heard or experienced it in journalism! David was already past me and stepping towards the field as I parsed together some words and mumbled across some combination of "good morning" and "good luck". I turned towards the press box but decided it may be best to go through this at the ground level so, I made my way behind the home team's bench.

Without a single warm-up, David trotted toward the middle of the field and in a business-like fashion gracefully adjust the football for the kickoff. With the speed of his mythical soccer scorchers but with the precision of a surgeon, he placed the opening kickoff at the one yard line where it appeared to be shot dead out of the sky and land in bounds. The opposing team's, kickoff returner fell on top of the ball like a small child making a belly flop into a pool. After a small pile on, the visiting team started to bring their offense onto the field in the end zone and David walked off the field as if he had done this a thousand times before.

I made notes about the thoughts I was feeling and little non-game details I was observing. This event would be a very different football story today. This issue was well beyond passing and rushing yards and scores. David sat on the bench for the half, looking as unimpressed as the rest of us at what was transpiring on the field. The first half was uneventful as the teams battled between the forty yard lines and neither coach was moved to have their kickers attempt a field goal from that distance. They trotted into their respective locker rooms at halftime with no points being recorded for either side.

As the teams departed the field, I saw my good friend Ron who was officiating, walking off. I stopped to ask him for some details. He said he had just a second to chat – "Eddie, the senior kicker, was doing some parkour moves at practice on Thursday and broke his ankle. That's all I know. Not a smart move for this kid." He didn't mention how David emerged into this situation and I grew even more curious as how to all these events had unfolded so quickly.

The halftime evaporated and the teams were back on the turf with the home team now receiving. As David continued to sit on the bench, I wondered how a kid who wasn't on the roster all season was eligible to play in their final game. I was able to chat with the defense line coach while the offense was on the field and he shared that, "David has been on the roster all season. He came out for summer practice and made the team but he didn't want to bump Eddie off in his senior season so he hasn't been with us. We need him now though with Eddie's accident." Talk about a good friend and a team player!

The game clock appeared to be moving expeditiously as each minute whisked by these evenly matched gridiron combatants. The punters at this point must have been exhausted as they were on the field as much as the regulars it seemed. The seconds went down to zero and we headed for overtime.

The visiting team won the coin flip and chose to start on offense.

The rules here are all about a balanced approach in high school football. There isn't a sudden death situation as each team plays both offense and defense. It is at that point that the possession is over.

After one possession, the teams were still all tied up with donuts on the board.

The visiting team quickly finished up their next four downs in the second possession and unceremoniously marched back off the field.

The blue boys of fall headed to their opponents' 25-yard line to begin their next set of downs in this possession. They fumble and quickly recover on their first down. For their second down, the home team makes a breakaway running play that brings them all the way to midfield.

Building on some momentum, it is first and ten once again and after faking a passing block, the Tight End pushes off his back foot and then takes a couple steps forward. He heads out on a drag route, going about 4-5 yards past the line of scrimmage, then cuts inside to run parallel to the line of scrimmage. He receives the ball around the 46 yard line and with the secondary covering some deep routes from the receivers, he turns to head up the field where he's tackled around the 34 yard line. The crowd responds with an absolute frenzy. After three failed running attempts to move the ball closer to the goal, it is fourth and ten from the 34 yard line and decision time for the head coach.

Do you go for it from here or head into yet a third possession?

At this point, I'm happy, I only have to write about these scenarios as the crowd begins to cheer, "Go, go, go..." I reminisce back to my childhood, and my mother reading me "The Little Engine That Could" and their repetitive chants of "go" begins to rhythmically sound like its motto: "I-think-I-can" to me. As I'm having flashbacks down next to the field, the coach calls a timeout and huddles with his team. The crowd begins to elevate their cheers, and I could only imagine the echo effect occurring in the ear holes of the players' helmets.

In the huddle, the coach immediately taps his quarterback on the helmet and he runs off the field. He heads in the direction of the bench and takes a quick knee in front of David. David, wearing Ronaldo's famous number 7 on his jersey, grabs his helmet and returns to the field for the first time since the kickoff. He keeps stride with the QB as they head back into the huddle. The coach and his receivers now head to the sidelines and the offense sets up for what is surely going to be a long field goal – the first ever FG attempt by David.

As if scripted in a storybook, the crowd goes completely silent.

David's father was the lone voice that rises above the solitude, "Você pode fazê-lo!" he shouts out to his son.

("You can do it" in Portuguese)

The center snaps the ball.

The QB acting as the holder receives it, places it down and David connects with the ball sending it clear through the field goal post into the parking lot and crashing through the windshield of the opposing team's bus.

If there was a radar gun on the kick it would have measured in excess of 80 miles per hour easily.

For a moment, the solitude remains as if the entire crowd was frozen in what they just witnessed.

The boys in blue storm the field along with their parents and families – they won.

THEY WON!

They had maintained their unblemished record in spite of losing their star kicker.

While I wasn't interested in reporting the stats on this from the beginning of this game, I did have a burning question that I needed answered.

The team and the crowd begins to chant "Mr. Football" and indeed "Mr. Futbol" had a bit of a name change that moment.

I made my way through the crowd and reached David in the end zone where he was with his Dad and his head coach. With one of the most genuine and sincere expressions, David turns to me and says "Hey Scoop, thanks again for coming to see me play."

For a second, I get a bit choked up thinking about this kid and all that he has just gone through and all that he went through losing his mother just a couple of years back. I reply, "David, what gave you the confidence to come back to the field?"

It was almost as if he expected me to ask this exact question.

He smiled innocently at me, looked around as if completely detached by the event that had just unfolded around him and the celebrations that were happening, and shared "It isn't soccer, Scoop, and the team really needed me. My Mom would have thought I could, and just like that story about that little engine, I thought I could."

That's clearly all the confidence he needed – he thought he could.

Distressed déjà vu

The German-born American poet, novelist and short story writer, Henry Charles Bukowski wrote, "We're all going to die, all of us, what a circus! That alone should make us love each other but it doesn't. We are terrorized and flattened by trivialities, we are eaten up by nothing." After this observation and until the time of his death from leukemia in 1994, I've often wondered if Bukowski ever felt differently. If I could speak to him now, I would tell him he was dead wrong (pun intended). Many of us are eaten up by everything or more appropriately, everything eats us up. Don't ever believe those with the false bravado, and the cocksure poker face that some play in this game of life. They may be navigating the art of overt diplomacy but in the midst of their concealed darkness and privately-held apprehensions, there's ample anxiety among these impudent and misguided souls that are in a constant conflict.

Bukowski would define me as either an outlier or at best a conundrum. The obvious flaw in my character has made my outward expression of love and trust for others as something to be lost, versus earned, when engaging new people. Am I the last of the hopeless romantics? At a younger age, some believed so. At this age, my expectations remain often very high for my fellow human beings and I am let down easily but that's a different story than the one being told this very day. This is a story of being terrorized and flattened by premonitions and not any premonition but that associated specifically with the passing of a loved one.

For it is this cross that I bear in this life.

These are two events that have happened in my lifetime that are worth sharing with you.

The first time in my life I could recall I was really distressed with the dying process and death was the night my maternal grandmother passed away. Odd as it may seem, I wasn't in the need of hearing the news of her passing through my nine year old ears. As our neighbor, who was staying with us that evening, fumbled to try to explain it all to me, she really didn't need to share a word. I didn't even need my parents' expression of such grief and sorrow when I saw them the next morning. I knew that she died, before she actually did. It caused me to become discombobulated and there was no easy explanation for what I had experienced.

As a nine year old, I sensed anticipation of, or anxiety over what was to be a future event – what many label as a presentiment, or a forewarning in modern day paranormal episodes of late afternoon television talk shows. I had no special insight, prompting or training. Beyond my Catholic-school understanding of the announcement of the incarnation by the angel Gabriel to Mary, I didn't have much experience or any other relevant example to draw from. The passing of my grandmother is what clearly brought forth this bold insight.

I knew.

I empirically knew she was going to die that night and it is as vivid in my mind today as it was that night when our neighbor told me to go to bed.

I knew because my grandmother came to tell me.

It wasn't a ghostly appearance like in Charles Dickens' A Christmas Carol. As I recall it now, she called my name, kissed the top of my forehead, gave me the biggest hug I have ever received and told me she would see me again sometime in the future. I wasn't despondent seeing her, at least at first, but for the three decades since that moment I was intimidated by the dying process and ultimately with any death.

The loss of my maternal grandmother at such a young age made me love my surviving grandparents that much more, but there was a gaping void that was left. Without her in our lives and in my life, our days were much different than they were before. Yes, it ate at me day after day and I maintain that I am remiss that I was never able to say goodbye to her as I had hoped.

Fast forward about fifteen years, I was driving home in the evening during the early part of Thanksgiving week and sensed that there was something that just didn't feel right. I had an uneasy feeling. I was not dizzy or nauseous, but I was vexatious and feeling completely out of alignment.

Upon arriving home, there was nothing out of the ordinary.

My parents and younger sister all went to bed early. Our German Shepherd was also already well into her canine dreamscape chasing squirrels or overindulging on some sizable beef or bison femur bone. For me, I decided it may be a healthier choice to also get some additional rest with the night before Thanksgiving alumni unofficial reunion festivities quickly approaching, and of course, the annual Turkey Bowl on Thanksgiving morning.

It must have been just before midnight when the hallway light beamed under my closed bedroom door. I heard my Father's voice speaking at a level above his normal calm and composed demeanor. The buckle on his belt was clanging as he fumbled to hold the phone and put his denim jeans on that were already hanging on the bannister outside of his door. As if we had planned it, my sister and I each opened our bedroom doors simultaneously as my parents were already heading down the stairs. "Your grandmother is being taken to the hospital – we'll meet you there," my Dad said as he seemingly leapt down the entire flight of stairs and out through the front door in a single motion.

Without hesitating, my sister and I changed clothes and we were in the car behind our parents heading towards the hospital. In the few moments that I did sleep, I already knew my paternal grandmother had already passed. My sister began to ask me a series of diagnostic questions. I listened, but I didn't share with her that I already knew what had transpired. There were few secrets we withheld from each other during our childhood or young adulthood but I didn't think she was ready to hear that I knew our grandmother had already died before anyone had shared the news of her being taken to the hospital.

We raced through the toll and across the bridge in what seemed like seconds. When we arrived at the emergency room, my grandfather, parents and aunt and uncle were already with my grandmother's body. My sister and I walked into the scene and it was all just déjà vu to me. I had already been there and lived out the entire scenario – I was an eyewitness to the event as it unfolded.

As my uncle detailed what transpired earlier that day with my grandmother's catheterization procedure and the uncomfortable feeling she was having when she returned home, I heard the words he was saying but confidently knew already what she had experienced.

When the emergency room attending, cardiologist and cardiology fellow met with our family, I felt a deep sense that I already knew what they had tried and what they didn't try when trying to save her. I turned to the fellow and shared that I knew that she tried to do everything that they could.

Yes, it was a flippant statement.

I knew that they didn't and knew that their lack of effort resulted in this unfortunate outcome.

As far as Bukowski and his nonsensical statement, these were not trivialities in my life and each of these events have made me love that much more as I have been gifted this astuteness where others ignore such invitations to see.

A discrepant schism

Many grade school science experiments stress the importance of observation as a primary objective. One observation by NASA recently was of little surprise to those of us that are experiencing the heat – that global temperatures so far this year are much higher than in the first half of 2015. Beyond this announcement, global warming and climate change experts employed at the top scientific companies and academic institutions have warned society for decades of the potential risks and impact of our actions (and inaction).

Researchers across the world observed the vast range of climatic changes occurring around us. There were those focused on the environment specific to the Arctic climate (i.e., remote sensing of ice and snow, snow cover and glacier mass/extent as indicators of climate change). Emerging theories and data as to atmospheric science, the elevation of greenhouse gases and the topic of the threats to the depleted ozone became commonplace in the nightly network news' weather reports. The public radio and public broadcast channels aired special reports on the economic and social impacts and C-SPAN would offer extended coverage of congressional hearings and presentations on current and proposed energy and environmental policy. In terms of water, the U.S. media would dichotomize the topic and offer drought coverage in California with flooding stories in the Southeast (largely from hurricanes and tropical storms) as if to balance the two ends of the spectrum somehow.

Several other researchers opted to focus on how best to prepare for adapting to the effects of climate change and how to harness technology to continue to advance society. Their collective observations and recommendations received equal praise as well as condemnation from the opposition. While some countries offered token gestures in the last few years and others signed global accords like The Paris Agreement, no research or policy would have prepared any of them for this singular, unforeseeable event that would quite literally expose all of their nescient lives.

The remaining survivors of Kristallnacht (or the Night of Broken Glass) which took place from November 9 to November 10, 1938 could recount a similar modulation on a much more local scale. Many were only small, impressionable children at the time but they could recall the execrable sights and the discordant sounds of Nazis in Germany destroying and torching synagogues and vandalizing Jewish businesses and homes. Parts of the population who experienced earthquakes and other natural disasters were all too familiar with the sonance. Those eyewitnesses and victims to terrorist attacks and other explosions shuddered at the jarring cacophony.

In an abrupt earth-shattering burst of sound, all the transparent glass across the globe fractured and splinted at once and then bizarrely disappeared.

In the seconds that followed many immediately thought some tremor or solar flare may have been the cause of the sonic boom. Some quickly questioned why did all of the fragments proceed to disappear. A few people wondered if perhaps it was the failure of some major acoustic weapon testing. The thought of a large-scale military-type weapon, similar in concept to the vehicle-mounted active denial system (V-MADS), that some government was experimenting with to possibly destroy an asteroid or some other rogue intention.

The hourglass didn't just run out figuratively, it died quite literally as every hourglass dematerialized.

The well-contained water in every aquarium and fish tank and all their aquatic inhabitants were washed away.

Windows in every apartment, church, commercial building and home vanished.

Glass eyewear of every kind from bifocals to reading to sunglasses seemed to explode off of the wearers' faces and every wristwatch quickly evolved to truly timeless timepieces.

Every bottle from the rarest of wines like that of Screaming Eagle Cabernet 1992 to the smallest batch of locally brewed craft beer were turned into worthless puddles in a matter of seconds.

Like the beginnings of glass making in Ireland that has been lost in the mists of time, every Waterford crystal bowl or vase to every household mixing or salad bowl were now lost to history.

It was if John Philip Sousa was conducting "Stars and Stripes Forever" for a reality show of exploding items in your kitchen, many household items burst and disintegrated in the midst of their owners from clocks and cups to lightbulbs and mirrors.

Visitors touring El Capitan in Yosemite had their lenses shatter on their Canon EOS 70D and photographers and video journalists saw through a bit clearer lens for the first time.

Selfie takers in Times Square had their cell phone and other mobile devices shatter in syncopation with the digital signage above their heads.

The Palm House at Schönbrunn Palace Park in Vienna rained down its 45,000 sheets of greenhouse glass on its enclosed plant kingdom.

Under its large glass dome, banquet guests in the Royal Lounge at the Hotel Negresco in Nice witnessed both the roof of the majestic ballroom and its spectacular Baccarat 16,309-crystal chandelier, moving it from a historical monument to historical memory.

Every mode of transportation lost its benefit of weather and wind protection as windshields made a crinkle sound and violently detonated in every country road running through quaint hamlets to the superhighways supporting the densely populated road warriors.

Throughout the aisles of Costco, Best Buy and in man caves everywhere, high-definition television screens fell off into obscurity.

Computers and monitors on every continent that have a matte plastic-coated screen were among the few devices spared.

Scientists to surgeons bemoaned their loss of microscopes and astrophysicists to cosmologists were brought to tears with the loss of their telescopes.

The spectacle had caused overwhelming damage to billions of people and property.

While we had observed so much, we now had an unfiltered view of our lives and all of those around us.

We were exposed in many new ways and to replace what we had loss would limit our new found transparency. For so long, glass was responsible for countless facets of the modern life and now, we would need to turn to the bountiful benefits of plastic and other innovative materials to sustain us and our visibility while sacrificing so much. One former hedge fund manager was quoted as stating "Not to be sarcastic but glass is now a break from our past. We'll be better off with betting on plastic. You can thank or blame me later."

An Intuitive Cache

As a kleiner junge (small boy) growing up in Germany, I had heard the stories of the ancient Greeks' view of our world. Unlike his contemporaries of the day, the Athenian philosopher Plato knew the Earth was a sphere. The entire universe, every star and planet, were suspended around us as "crystal spheres". When I was a bit older, in my schooling I had read more about this in the "Myth of Er" in his book, "The Republic".

Plato's student Aristotle also later wrote about this "geocentric model" but it was Eudoxus of Cnidus, whom I recollect, that first worked out a mathematical-based demonstration of uniform circular motion with Plato. Claudius Ptolemy advanced Aristotelian physics even further, but I won't be boring you with more of a celestial history lesson any more. For my recollection here is of my own childhood growing up in Germany. I wish to share with you an encounter that is far more terrestrial in nature, though perhaps by the end you will consider this event to be somewhat phenomenal regarding our world and your place in it.

My village outside of Arbergen and our home weren't anything remarkable. The timber-framed structure of my childhood home combined our living quarters, stalls and hay storage all under one roof. This Fachhallenhaus or Low German house is the quintessential rustic, agricultural farmhouse style that you are likely well familiarized. From the 13th century until today, there have been alternative names but the German style endures. There wasn't much in the way of change in my life up until the point when a German-Italian family became our newest neighbors. The lovely couple had two daughters. I became infatuated at first sight with one and her chestnut brown eyes and hair.

My first interaction with her was beyond awkward. She walked past me in the market and instead of saying hello or introducing myself, I blurted, "Was suchen sie?" (What are you looking for?)

She replied, "Alles."

Everything?

She was looking for everything?

I thought to myself who looks for everything and how much could be found here in the market.

She wasn't making any sense to me or maybe was being just a little foolish. Thinking I should revert back to a more conventional introduction, I extended my hand and announced, "I am your neighbor and my name is Heinrich Wilhelm Matthias Olbers."

The earth ceased spinning and time seemingly stopped as she looked at me with her warm, rich eyes that were like German sweet chocolate, closed them for a brief second, and laughed right at me. "Well, Heinrich Wilhelm Matthias Olbers," she declared, "I'm Ermelinda, and I am also your new neighbor."

I knew Ermelinda was clearly an Italian name but it cleverly contains Germanic elements – ermen, which means "whole, universal" and linde, which means "soft, tender".

In German, I offered, "Are you really, looking for, uh, for everything?"

"Yes, but I already see most of it," she informed me.

In a few mere seconds of speaking to Ermelinda, I went from the new neighbor to being in love to now being completely perplexed.

I was confused and didn't know how to respond to her comment of being able to see most of it.

Well, what was she looking for if she could already see it?

Maybe, the better question would be to ask her, what is "it" exactly?

"Ermelinda?" I asked, "what exactly is "it" that you already see?" S
he turned directly in front of me, her eyes staring nearly through mine and admitted, "When I close my eyes I can see everything in the entire universe."

"Like Galileo or Copernicus?" I questioned.

"Yes, I can see everything on this planet, in this solar system and in the universe," she exclaimed. "I just need to close my eyes and concentrate."

"So you can see Jupiter's moons like Galileo did?"

"Yes."

"What is my the name of my rindfleisch (beef cow)?

"It doesn't work that way. I can see you have a cow but I don't know it's name."

"Oh!" I nodded.

"Is the universe you can see finite or infinite?"

Ermelinda looked at me completely puzzled but she didn't answer.

She turned away for a moment and then back toward me, but again didn't answer.

Her mouth opened slightly, but she didn't say anything more except for a mild sigh.

"I believe all the dark areas of the sky mean that the universe is finite," I informed her. "I'm going to be an astronomer and I'm going prove this."

Ermelinda gave me no reply. She grabbed my hands, closed her eyes and just smiled.

The cardboard cogitation

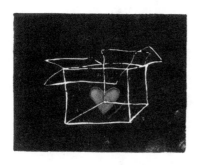

Paizlee questioned Daxten's intentions on a daily basis. *I just don't know what he's thinking – I mean what he's REALLY thinking,* she thought.

While the college classmates had only known each other a few months, they now found their lives intertwined. They found that working together in the produce section of their town's local supermarket allowed for some of their deepest conversations over everything from cabbage to carrots. In spite of their developing discourse that extended well beyond the market's hours, they had never been to each other's homes, and they never shared any intimate thoughts about current or past relationships.

While there was never any talk of anything resembling spiritual nosegays or permanence, the topic of conversation ranged from debating the value of bizarre food oddities like the summertime shack in Narragansett that cooks clam cakes in beef fat to proposing and adding new exotic journeys to their never-ending travel bucket list like their shared passion to travel to Mongolia's forbidden zone to find Genghis Khan's tomb.

On one hand, he would indeed be a great travel companion but even when his lips are moving and sharing so much, there's something much deeper he's not sharing with me.

She was also puzzled watching Daxten pile paper packaging and cardboard cartons in the cabin and cargo bed of his rusted-up, old, white with red pinstripe, 1975 International 150 pickup truck at the end of every shift. She pondered why he needed to procure all of these materials but she was too shy to pry, and far too befuddled to inquire about his peculiar hoarding habits. She observed that "Dax" (as she nicknamed him) didn't discriminate about size, shape, color, or texture of the boxes. He also didn't care much for the prior content – it simply didn't matter to Dax if the carton previously held garlic or grapes. Don't the stains or remnants in the boxes have an odor, she imagined.

It wasn't until Paizlee spied on Dax doodling in their Abnormal Psychology class did she gain a valuable insight into one of his private obsessions.

Is that a room he is sketching?

Is it a cube?

Surely, it resembles one of the hundreds of cartons he has taken out of the store.

But wait, is it a box within a box? I am so confused!

As Paizlee got lost in her thoughts, Dax tilted his head towards her as if he was eavesdropping into her mind. He then pulled his hands under his desktop almost to offer her a clearer view of his sketches. She pretended not to be interested, flicked her wrists outwards, and faked a pronounced yawn behind her guarded smile.

With class literally drawing to close, Paizlee gathered her backpack and books and darted for the rear door to the classroom hoping to avoid any awkwardness with Dax.

It was too late.

Dax stopped her midway to the door and slyly asked, "So, did you like what you saw?"

Okay, think something clever and let's avoid discussing this right now.

"Sure, well, uh…I thought the graph Professor shared on biological causal factors and also the table listing all the imbalances of neurotransmitters and hormones made me feel like I had all of those – but that's every Abnormal Psych class here," Paizlee replied.

"No, not that, you know, my sketch you were fixated on," said Dax.

"Ohhh, were you doodling something? I thought you were just taking notes." *That was a close one!*

"C'mon, be honest, you saw my room."

"Room? Is that what that was? I thought it was box in a box or a cube or something."

Oops. What just happened? I did just admit to seeing his sketches.

Ugh, nice move.

She shrugged her shoulders while looking at Dax quizzically. "You need to see it, it is nearly done," blurted Dax, "I want you to come to my house to see it. How about after class – right before we have to go to work? Please? I really want to share this with you."

I couldn't believe what he was saying. This person was the same guy who had been sending me mixed signals since we met. I was pretty sure we were firmly in the friend zone.

Was this response his big move? Not very sophisticated at all.

"Sounds like a plan – see you later, Dax."

When I got to the corner of Maple Avenue and made the left turn down his one-way street I could feel my heart beating out of the Incubus logo emblazoned across the t-shirt on my chest. His house was about three-quarters of the way down the street. It was a yellow, two-story home with what appeared to be a full attic. I wondered for a moment which was his bedroom and then refocused my thoughts on where I should park my car. Dax's truck was neatly tucked in the unusually formed driveway next to his father's work van. They had apparently cut the curb extra wide on the street in front of what was clearly another lot his family owned. The only available spot on the street was blocking him in – a risk I was willing to take just to see him and his "big reveal" as soon as possible.

I didn't realize while I was performing it but Dax was standing at his half-screen front door observing and laughing at my "expert" parallel parking maneuvers. He met me on the concrete paver path to his door while shaking his head and continuing to laugh heartily at my expense.

Okay, laugh it up.

Dax grabbed Paizlee's hand and they darted up the creaky wooden stairs to the second floor apartment that he shared with his parents.

As he flung open the door, he spun Paizlee in a 180 degree U-turn and headed up another flight of stairs. Paizlee wasn't expecting Dax to grab her hand in the first place, let alone make these parkour moves around staircases and doors. When they arrived up to the top of the second flight of stairs in what appeared to be a full-size, stand-up attic, it was lit only by the thin outline of late-afternoon sunlight that was peeking through the room-darkening shade on the far end of the room.

"Okay, close your eyes"

Close my eyes? It is dark in here as it is.

"Ok, my eyes are closed."

"Don't peek!"

At what? The dark? Geez, Dax.

"Got it. Ok...Dax."

"Okay, open them."

As if by a cosmic coincidence, I could hear the faint sound of U2's "Tryin' to Throw Your Arms Around the World" as Dax placed his hand now on my shoulder. I opened my eyes and saw the cardboard-patchwork monstrosity that took up more than half of the attic room. Amidst the interwoven colors and logos of every hijacked used blueberry box to quite literally every detergent brand and napkin packaging and tissue box with yellow and blue in its color scheme, I could make out a domed-like structure resembling Vincent Van Gogh's "Starry Night".

"Just wait for what comes next, Paizlee!"

I was already in awe of his creativity and willingness to share this beautiful piece of artwork.

Dax disappeared for a moment.

I laughed to myself as I heard him flip a switch after stumbling over what sounded like a large, rigid, cardboard box.

I was quite literally stunned.

Piercing through strategically-placed holes within the surrounding image were mini holiday lights that illuminated the scene like a planetarium. Dax's cardboard Van Gogh creation came magically to life.

As I stood in the middle of the room turning around and around to appreciate every angle and every little detail, Dax grabbed both of my hands, leaned into me and whispered in my right ear, "I…I created all of this for you. I recall one of the first days I saw you, you had a white shirt with the Starry Night image on it. I wanted to build this to show you how much I…I, well, really like you."

I guess I finally found out what he was thinking all along – it was me.

I was his muse and he was thinking only of me.